MW00982452

Wherever Bears Be

A Story for Two Voices

by Sue Ann Alderson
Pictures by Arden Johnson

Tricycle Press
Berkeley, California

TRICYCLE PRESS
P.O. Box 7123
Berkeley, California 94707

Published simultaneously in Great Britain by Tradewind Books Limited, 30B Princes Avenue, London N10 3LR
and in Canada by Tradewind Books Limited, 2216 Stephens Street, Vancouver, British Columbia, V6K 3W6

Book design by Susan Van Horn

Library of Congress Cataloging-in-Publication Data
Alderson, Sue Ann.
Wherever bears be / by Sue Ann Alderson; pictures by Arden Johnson.
p. cm.
Summary: Two girls embark on a berry-picking expedition, unaware that
they are being followed by bears.
ISBN 1-883672-77-5
[1. Blueberries—Fiction. 2. Bears—Fiction.] I. Johnson-Petrov, Arden, ill.
II. Title.
PZ7.A3617Wh 1999
[E]—dc21 98-34405
CIP
AC

First printing, 1999

Printed in Hong Kong

1 2 3 4 5 6 — 03 02 01 00 99

For my parents, Gene and Ruth Hartley, and for Rebecca, Kai, Tobi, Wendy, Steve, Fiona—my family, wherever they be. —S.A.

For my wise daughter Alisa. May you find the berry patch of your dreams. –A.J.

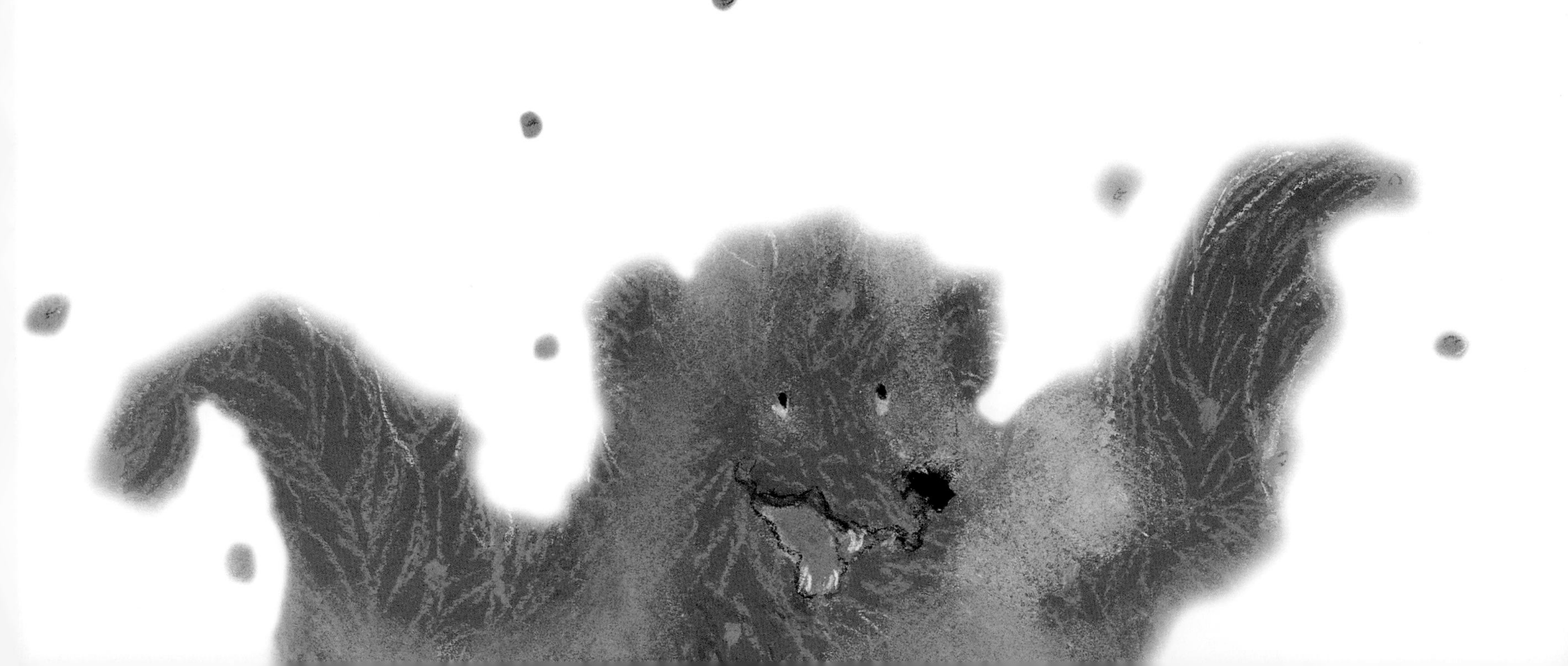

"We have to pick blueberries high on the mountain, Belinda, you and I. I wish we didn't. Sloggy old mountain. Sloggy Belinda."

"Sloggy Samantha!"

"Keep up, Belinda!"

"Keep up yourself!"

"I wish we'd find one bush so full of berries,
we'd be done in a wink.
I wish mountains were flat! I wish all of that!
This path slogs up and up."

"It does!"

"These trees are thick with
the thought of bears..."

"Bears?"

"...bears hungry for berries."

*"Hi, bears, wherever
bears be."*

"I'll make up a song,
to hold the bears back:

Fiddle-dee-di, fiddle-dee-dee, stay away, bears, wherever

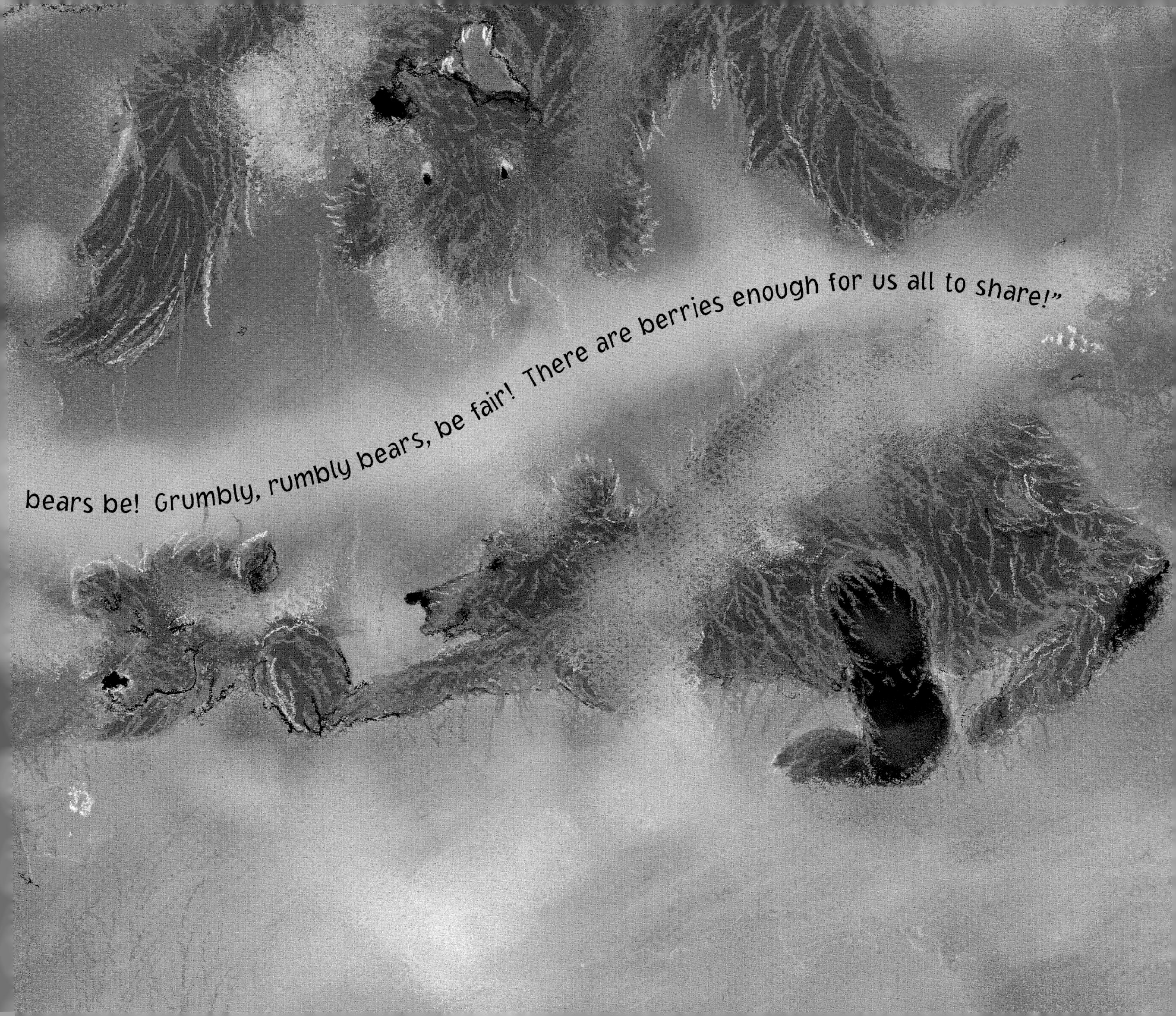

bears be! Grumbly, rumbly bears, be fair! There are berries enough for us all to share!"

“Belinda! Stop eating them all!
Slow work, this picking.
Bears lurk about when the picking is slow.”

"Smash-crash! In the brush!"

"Over where?"

"There! There!"

"Yes! That's a bear!"

"You think that's a bear?"

“But now I see—no, a squirrel sounds loud
when the picking is slow!”

"Here's a stream and a bridge—
thump-a-bump-run!"

"Thump-a-bump-run!"

"Belinda, why are you plashing berries
over the side?"

"To see the water circle."

"Slap-splash under the bridge—can a bridge hide a bear?"

"Bears can go hiding any old where!"

"But no, now I see—
a raccoon-splash sounds like
a bear-splash to me!"

"Should we go further? Do we dare?
We're all alone. Just us and maybe a bear?
What's that shadow? See it rear?"

"Yes, yes!"

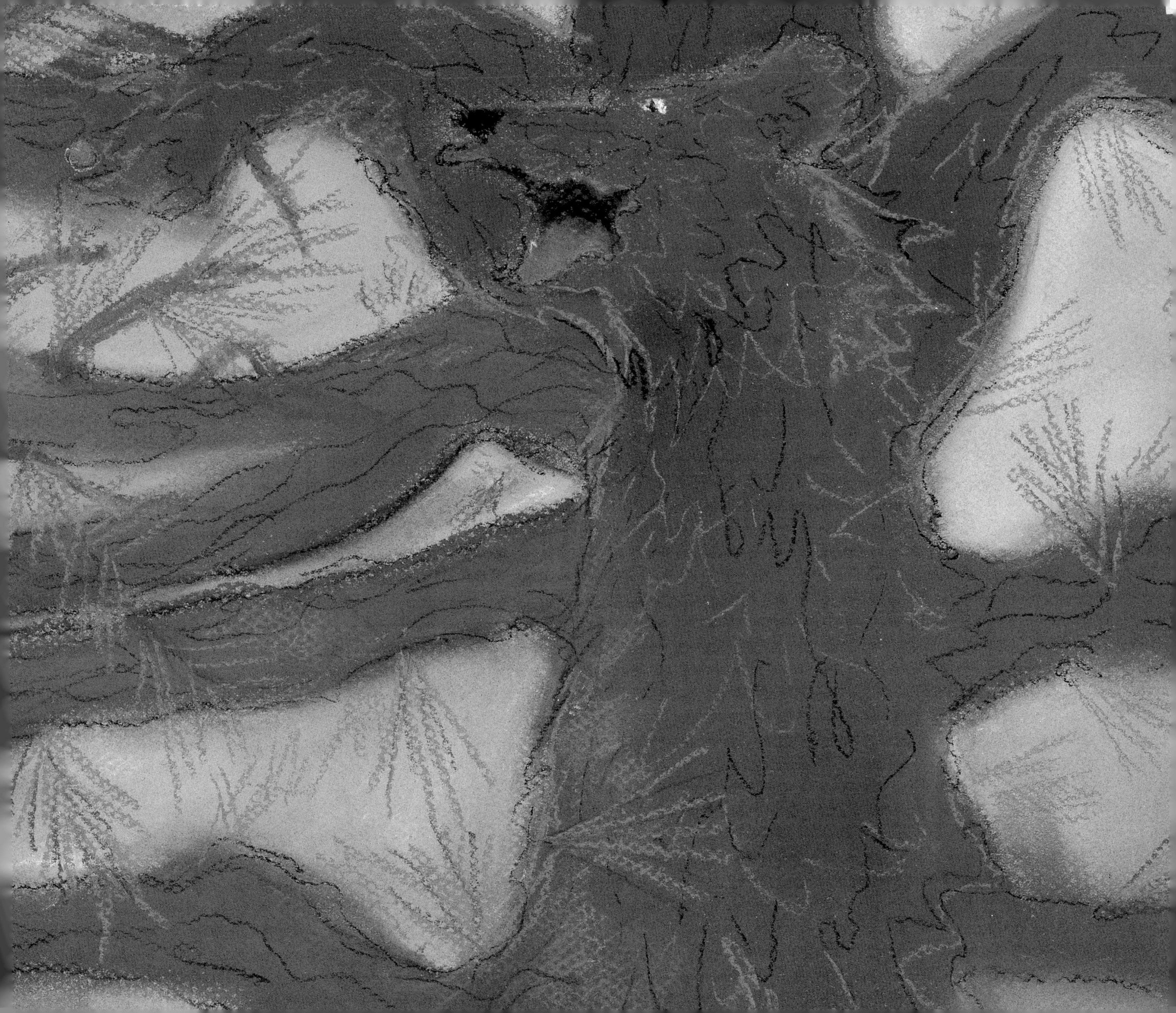

"But now I see—no,
it's only a deer turning to go."

"At last, here's the top! Are there berries about?"
"Yes! Buckets of berries!"
"We'll pick our pots full..."
"...and leave lots for the bears!"

“Now I almost wish I could see
the bears come, having fun.
I’ll sing a new song
so the bears will know:

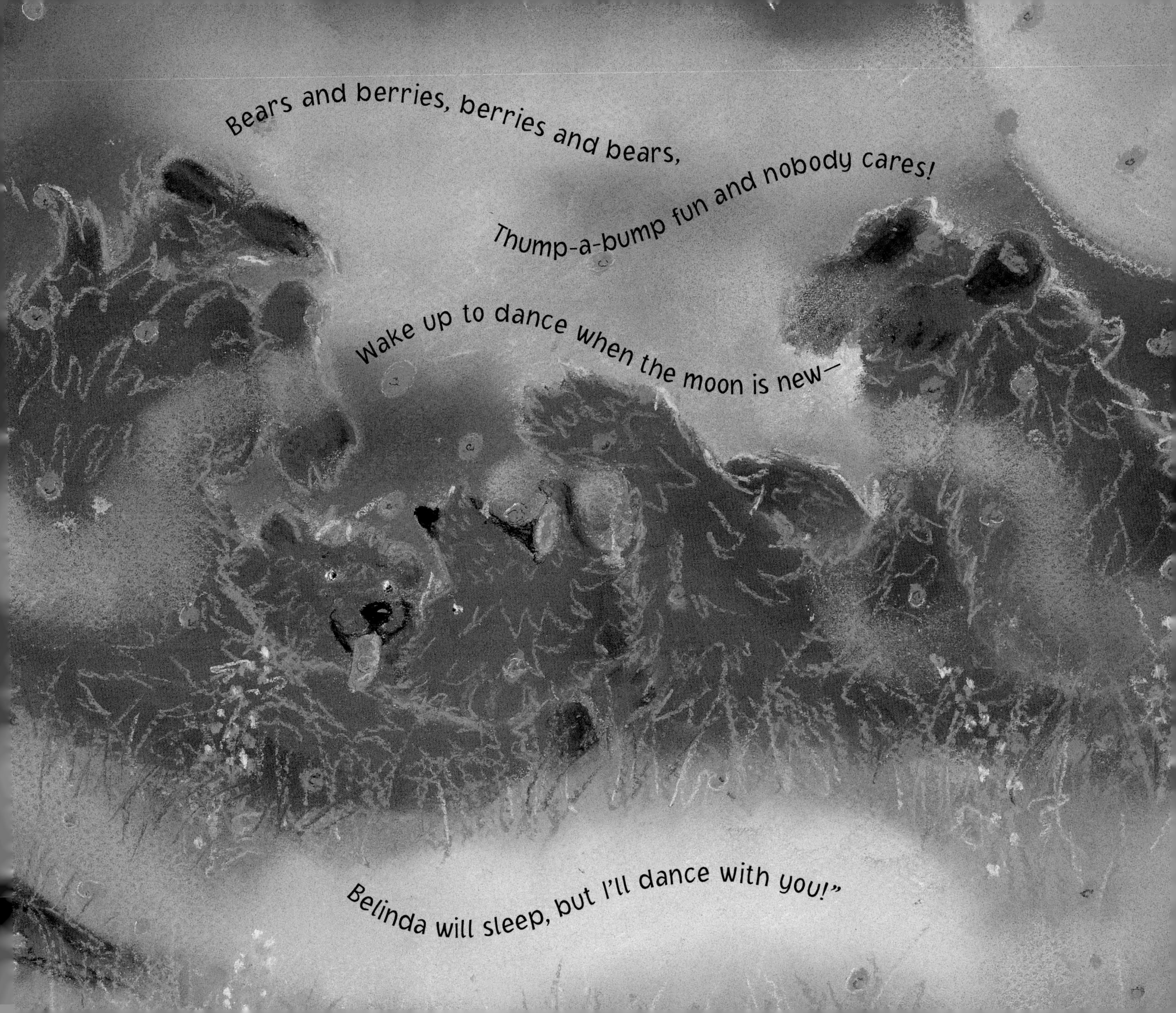

Bears and berries, berries and bears,

Thump-a-bump fun and nobody cares!

Wake up to dance when the moon is new—

Belinda will sleep, but I'll dance with you!"

"Oops! Whoops! Why, I've banged my pot on its side,
spilled my berries! Oh, no! Almost half!"

"Don't cry! I'll help! There, your pot is almost full again!"

"Thanks, Belinda.
Maybe then I will wake you
so you can come too..."

"If the bears dance at night?"

"Yes, that's what I'll do!"

“We have so many berries that even you have some left in your tin pot, Belinda. Now let’s go home, past trees thick with the hush of no bears. They’ve all gone berry-picking some other where.”

"Bye, bears,
wherever bears be!"